W9-DAO-008

Literal Lily

Written by Kate Hanscom

Illustrations by Lynda Hanscom

Maura -
I hope that Lily
brings a smile
to your face!
Happy Reading!
Kate Hanscom

Ambassador International
GREENVILLE, SOUTH CAROLINA & BELFAST, NORTHERN IRELAND

www.ambassador-international.com

Literal Lily

ISBN: 978-1-62020-118-3
eISBN: 978-1-62020-169-5

Illustrations: Lynda Hanscom
Cover design and typesetting: Matthew Mulder
E-book conversion: Anna Riebe

AMBASSADOR INTERNATIONAL
Emerald House
427 Wade Hampton Blvd.
Greenville, SC 29609, USA
www.ambassador-international.com

AMBASSADOR BOOKS
The Mount
2 Woodstock Link
Belfast, BT6 8DD, Northern Ireland, UK
www.ambassador-international.com

The colophon is a trademark of Ambassador

For my husband, Chris, and daughter, Allison

− Kate

For my husband, Doug, and daughter, Cara

− Lynda

Our heartfelt thanks to our family and friends for your continued
love, support and inspiration.

Lily slowly rubbed her eyes as she woke up. A smile spread across her face. Today was Girls' Day Out! First, she would go shopping with Mommy to get ready for her first day of school. After shopping, Lily and Mommy would eat lunch at Sammy's Sandwich Shop.

"Rise and shine, Lily!" Mommy said cheerfully. "Time to get up!"

Lily hopped out of bed, thinking hard about her mother's words. "Well, I have the *rise* part down. Now about the *shine*…"

Lily opened her closet and pulled out her bin of dress-up clothes. She grabbed her pink tutu and a dazzling tiara. She slipped her feet into spar-kle-farkle ruby red tap shoes. "I think all of these things shine!" Lily said as she looked at herself in the mirror.

"Good morning!" Lily chirped to her parents as she pranced into the kitchen in her fancy outfit.

"Lily, you look beautiful!" Daddy smiled as he kissed her on the forehead.

"Oh, Lily! How sparkly you are! What made you choose this outfit for our special shopping day?" Mommy asked.

"Well, you said to *rise and shine*. This is the best way that I know how."

"Oh, Lily!" Mommy chuckled. "I didn't mean to *literally* rise and shine!"

Lily looked thoughtful. "Mommy, what does *literally* mean?"

"To take something literally means to take something exactly as it is said, word for word," Mommy explained.

Lily thought for a moment. "Oh. I suppose I will change my outfit then."

After eating her toast and berries and brushing her teeth, Lily was ready to go. "Bye, Daddy! We love you!" Lily called as Mommy led her out the door.

Bye, girls," he called back. "Have fun! Shop 'til you drop!"

The car door slammed shut. Mommy and Lily dashed towards the mall. They rushed through the doors, delighted to start their shopping adventure.

All of a sudden, Lily fell to the ground with a great big KERPLOP. "Lily! Are you all right?" Mommy asked, helping Lily to her feet.

"Yes, Mommy, I am fine! Daddy told me to *shop 'til we drop*. That is what I was doing!"

"Oh, Lily!" Mommy said. "Daddy didn't literally mean to *shop 'til we drop*. He just meant that he hoped we would have fun shopping and find all the items that we are looking for."

"Well, that makes more sense," Lily said as she brushed herself off. A giddy grin spread across her face. "Let's go *shop 'til we drop!*"

First, Mommy and Lily went to the school supply store. There, they picked out a green backpack with pink and white polka-dotted straps. Then they chose pencils, crayons, and a bright blue folder.

Next, Mommy and Lily skipped into the clothing store. They found so many pretty things. Mommy clapped for Lily as she tried on outfits. Then they shopped for shoes. One pair made Lily dance!

All of a sudden, a voice shouted from behind them. "Lily? Is that you? I haven't seen you since you were a baby!" Both Lily and Mommy turned to see Mrs. Green. Her arms waved wildly as she hurried over to Lily.

"Mrs. Green, how are you?" Mommy asked.

"I'll be better when I give this little girl a kiss!" Mrs. Green replied. "She is so cute that I could just eat her right up."

"Ahhh!" Lily shrieked as she jumped behind Mommy's back. "Oh, Lily!" Mommy reached for her. "You remember Mrs. Green. She lives next door to Nana. Say hello," Mommy urged.

Lily gulped. Shyly, she peeked out from behind Mommy's back and whispered, "Hi, Mrs. Green."

"Sweetheart, what is wrong?" Mrs. Green asked.

Lily glanced at Mommy. "Well, tomorrow is my first day of school and… I don't want to be eaten up before I even get there!" she told Mrs. Green.

"Lily!" Mommy said softly. She pulled Lily out from behind her back. "Mrs. Green isn't *literally* going to eat you up! It's just a silly saying. It means she thinks you are adorable."

"Oh!" Lily said. She gave a sheepish look to Mrs. Green. "So, I shouldn't take what you said word for word."

"That's right," Mrs. Green explained. "I'm sorry to have scared you. I'm just so happy to see how you have grown."

After hugs, Mommy and Mrs. Green said goodbye. Lily took Mommy's hand and went to lunch.

"Are you hungry after all of our shopping?" Mommy asked. She opened a menu.

"Yes, I am very hungry!" Lily replied. The picture of a grilled cheese sandwich and a thick chocolate shake made her mouth water.

"I am too," Mommy said. "I'm so hungry I could eat a horse!"

Lily looked wide-eyed at Mommy. "You don't really mean…" she questioned.

"That's right," Mommy said with a nod. "I wouldn't *literally* eat a horse!"

Mommy and Lily chatted and laughed during lunch at Sammy's. Lily ate every bite of her sandwich. She slurped her milkshake. Soon it was time to go. Mommy and Lily gathered their bags. They thanked the waitress and headed home.

"How was shopping, girls?" Daddy greeted Mommy and Lily as they entered the front door, bags in tow.

"It was great!" Mommy replied.

"Yes! We really *shopped 'til we dropped!*" Lily said, chuckling to herself.

"Let me see what you purchased!" Daddy said. "I want to see a fashion show."

Lily trotted to her room to show off her new outfits. With each change of wardrobe, she walked out into the living room. There, she spun around to show Daddy each angle.

Then she pranced back to her room. At the end of the fashion show, they decided her new purple jumper was the perfect outfit for her first day of school.

Daddy helped Lily fill her backpack with her new school supplies. Together, they put away her new clothes. Then they played a game of hopscotch in the driveway.

After dinner, Lily took a bath. She wanted to be fresh and clean for the morning. As she brushed her teeth and put on her pajamas, she began to yawn.

"You have had a busy day, Little Miss," Mommy said to Lily as she and Daddy tucked her into bed.

"Yes, I had a great day! Thank you for all of my new things." Lily let out another long, sleepy yawn. As she got under her covers, they talked about the best parts of their day. Lily could drift to sleep with pleasant thoughts in her head.

Finally, as her droopy eyelids began to close, Mommy and Daddy each leaned in and gave Lily a kiss on the forehead. "Goodnight, Lily," Daddy spoke softly. "I love you from here to the moon!"

A sleepy smirk flitted across Lily's face. "Oh, Daddy, you don't mean that literally… word for word," she said. She was proud that she had finally understood her new word. "No one can love someone THAT much!"

Daddy gave her another kiss on the cheek. "Actually, Lily," he whispered, "this time I meant exactly what I said."

About the Author

Kate Hanscom grew up as the youngest of three children in Utica, New York. Her writing is inspired by the vivid and whimsical imagination that she has had since childhood, though the antics and stories of her youth have provided no lack of story material.

Currently, Kate lives in central Massachusetts with her husband, Chris, and daughter, Allison. A graduate of Stonehill College, she lives her life with a song in the background, a pen in her hand, and the belief that with hard work and a plan, anything is achievable.

In putting pen to paper, Kate is delighted to see the characters of her imagination come to life. She hopes that when readers meet *Lily*, they are encouraged to laugh, ask questions, expand their minds, and dream bigger than they ever knew possible!

About the Illustrator

Lynda Hanscom is originally from Long Island, New York. She holds a BFA from St. John's University and an MAT from the Rhode Island School of Design. As an art teacher, she guided hundreds of budding student artists from kindergarten through high school to be creative through drawing, painting, and sculpting.

Also the illustrator of *Tough Tommy*, a children's bereavement book, she now lives in Northern Connecticut with her very supportive husband, Doug. Lynda's inspiration and joy comes from her daughter, Cara; son, Chris, and his wife, Kate; and her sweet little granddaughter, Allison.

For more information about

KATE HANSCOM

&

LITERAL LILY

please visit:

www.katehanscom.com
www.facebook.com/katehanscomauthor

....

For more information about
AMBASSADOR INTERNATIONAL
please visit:

www.ambassador-international.com
@AmbassadorIntl
www.facebook.com/AmbassadorIntl